A LEARICAL LEXICON

A Learical Lexicon

from the works of Edward Lear
compiled by Myra Cohn Livingston
and with drawings by Joseph Low

A MARGARET K. MCELDERRY BOOK

Atheneum 1985 *New York*

Library of Congress Cataloging in Publication Data
Lear, Edward, 1812–1888.
  A Learical lexicon.
  "A Margaret K. McElderry Book."
  Summary: A glossary of humorous and nonsense words
featuring unusual spellings, hidden meanings, transposed
letters, and onomatopoeic sounds, selected from the letters
and other witty writings of the English author/artist.
    1. Lear, Edward, 1812–1888—Language—Glossaries, etc.—
—Juvenile literature.   2. Play on words—Juvenile litera-
ture.   3. English language—Anecdotes, facetiae, satire,
etc.—Juvenile literature.   [1. Lear, Edward, 1812–1888.
2. Play on words.   3. English language—Wit and humor]
I. Livingston, Myra, Cohn.   II. Low, Joseph, 1911–   ill.
PR4879.L2Z459   1985   821'.8   84–18635
ISBN 0–689–50318–0

Text copyright © 1985 by Myra Cohn Livingston
Illustrations copyright © 1985 by Joseph Low
All rights reserved
Published simultaneously in Canada by McClelland & Stewart, Ltd.
Composition by Maryland Linotype
Baltimore, Maryland
Printed by Connecticut Printers
First Edition

For J.L.—all four of you!

M.C.L.

For my three Learical girls

J.L.

ALSO BY MYRA COHN LIVINGSTON
AND JOSEPH LOW

A LOLLYGAG OF LIMERICKS
(A Margaret K. McElderry Book)

If you have ever been *scroobious* or *bebothered* or *debemisted* about the meaning of a word -if you like *boshblobberbosh* and the *mumbian* sound of words, you are *phortschnit* (fortunate, as Edward Lear once wrote) . . .

Because here are *vords* and *vorx of hart*, which Lear has *writtled*, and *piggchurs* by *nartist* Joseph Low to delight your *ize* . . .

And if you can *skriggle* through, from A to Z, no longer will you be *absquatulated* or *decompoged* or *befizzled*. You will merely *erjoice* that Edward Lear, *landskip* painter and nonsense writer, played with words.

Edward Lear was a remarkable man whose *wurble inwentions* attest to his determination to overcome handicaps and to fight dull reason and convention with humor and imagination. Born in 1812 in England, the twenty-first of twenty-two children, a victim of asthma and epilepsy, he began to earn his own living at sixteen. His dream of becoming a renowned landscape painter during his lifetime never came true. He is best remembered for the limericks and story-poems, the nonsense drawings he made and stories he wrote in his twenties for the children and grandchildren of a rich patron and, later, for children of friends and others he met during his many travels.

Lear put some of his nonsense words, like the *Bong Tree*, the *Chankly Bore*, and the *Gromboolian Plain*, and exclamations, like *Timbaloo and Tilly-loo*, into his story-poems. But it was in his letters to friends that he introduced a variety of words with unusual spellings and hidden meanings. Some words transposed letters, like *erjoice* for *rejoice* or *buplisher* for *publisher*. Some words not only mixed up letters but replaced particular letters of the alphabet with others, *ossifers* for *officers* or *dragging* for *dragon*. Lear delighted in phonetic spelling—*fizzicle* for *physical, bizzy* for *busy*, and *mortle* for *mortal*. Many words carried onomatopoetic sounds, like *meloobious* and *growlygrumble*. Others affected Greek spellings, like *phogg* for fog and *fax* for facts. Some words could be changed in meaning by a twist of imagination: *stircumsance* for circumstance, *Bundy* for Sunday. Other words he left to the imagination of the reader— *grisogorious, blumphious* and *ompsiquillious.*

There are many people whose childhood years are no happier than were Edward Lear's. Often these men and women sit about and complain, *begloomed* about what they did not have when they were young. It was Lear's belief that humor, hope and imagination help to overcome many of life's frustrations and sorrows. It is in this spirit that *A Learical Lexicon* has been compiled, with the added hope that its readers will welcome a *nopportunity* to create other *wurble inwentions* of their own!

mcl

A man among strangers longs to hear and to speak his own language. Many times I have taken one of Lear's books from the shelf, opened it anywhere, and settled down for a chat. That is what these drawings are: not an imitation of his speech, but a conversation between friends.

jl

A a

APPY

Wots the hods so long as ones appy?

ALOOKING

So I must e'en turn over another stone as the sandpiper said when he was alooking for vermicules.

B b

BEBOTHERED

. . . bebothered and boshed.

BILED

CARROTABLE

So I sold the poor old place, and it now belongs to the highly pious and exalted Miss Macdonald Lockhart, who has bought it for some carrotable institootion.

CURLY BURLY

. . . that curly burly woman.

DIRTYISSIMO

This place is vastly dirty. Dirtyissimo.

DEBBLES

EQUAL-NOXIOUS

The winter seems all gone for the present—though the Equal-noxious gales will doubtless come in disgustable force. . . .

EXTASY

. . . several bad accidents have happened by people injuring their brains from standing on their heads in an extasy of delight, before these works of art.

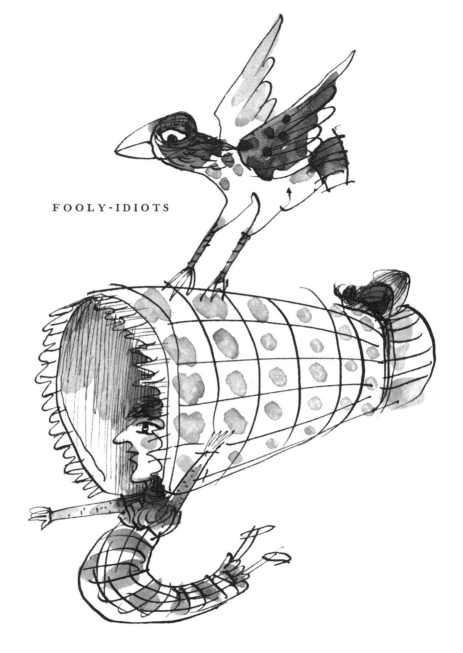

FOOLY-IDIOTS

FOOLY-IDIOTS

. . . fooly-idiots of fashion.

FRIZZ

The cold is so great that my nose is frizz so hard that I use it as a paper cutter.

G g

GNATURAL

O my child! here is a gnat! which, the window being open, is but gnatural. So I shuts up both vinder and letter, and goodbye.

GROMPHIBBEROUS

Its Coast scenery may truly be called pomskizillious and gromphibberous, being as no words can describe its magnificence.

HOPPOSIT

Now, this letter will neither be a nice one nor a long one, but, just the hopposit for it is to say I am coming to England fast as I can, . . .

HENNEMIES

. . . boxed up here in the middel of hennemies.

HUNAPPY

HENNYBODDY

The head waiter is a praiseworthy individual, & his efforts to make a goose go round 18 diners were remarkable . . . "Who's this for?" said an agitated buttony boy . . . "HENNYBODDY!" said the waiter in a decided tone . . .

ICIE

ICIE

How frigid that icie ladye was no Polar or N. Zemblan tongue can tell!

IJIOT

For all that one forlorn ijiot said—"Is that a *Palm*-tree Sir?"—"No," replied I quietly,—"it is a Peruvian Brocoli."

JIBBEROLTER

J j

JIBBEROLTER

It is orfle cold here, and I don't know what to do. I think I shall go to Jibberolter, passing through Spain, and doing Portigle later.

JURNLES

. . . I trust . . . to the benefit obliquely of many of my felly creatures who will hereafter peeroase my jurnles, and admyer my pigchers.

KNOCK-SHOCK-SPRAIN

K k

KNOCK-SHOCK-SPRAIN

The knock-shock-sprain which I got in that Southampton train bothered me a good deal . . .

KNOWNOTHINGATALLABOUTWHATONEIS-GOINGTODO-NESS

You see therefore in how noxious a state of knownothing-atallaboutwhatoneisgoingtodo-ness I am in.

LANDSKIP

LANDSKIP

. . . a wonderfully lovely view over the river Temms & the surroundiant landskip.

LITHOGROFIGGING

. . . sketches of Corfû for separate lithogrofigging, & sale here .

MILINGTARY

MILINGTARY

. . . and I saw V(ictor) E(mmanuel) quite closely, as well as all the milingtary specktickle.

MUCILAGINOUS

I have pretty well made up my mucilaginous mind to cross to Liverpool to-night.

NINFERNAL

. . . four hundred and seventy-three cats at least are all at once making a ninfernal row in the garden close to my window. Therefore, being mentally decompoged, I shall write no more.

NOKKING

Here's somebod a nokking at the dolorous door.

OSHUN

OSHUN

. . . I embark on the oshun . . .

ORANG OUTANGS

What do you think of a society for clothing and educating by degrees the Orang outangs?

PARTICKLY

. . . the food is good generally, but partickly trout and lobsters . . .

PHITS

. . . phits of coffin . . .

QUEET

Q q

QUEET

"Here be tew litters zur: —the boy is all queet drewndid . . ."

QUANGLE WANGLE

On the top of the Crumpetty Tree
    The Quangle Wangle sat

ROZIZ

R r

ROZIZ

And if you voz to see my roziz
As is a boon to all men's noziz,—
You'd fall upon your back and scream—
"O Lawk! O criky! it's a dream!"

RARD HUN

Meanwhile, I must go & try & birculate my clood, by a
rard hun on the righ hoad.

SPLITMECRACKLE

SPLITMECRACKLE

A vile beastly rottenheaded foolbegotten brazenthroated pernicious piggish screaming, tearing, roaring, perplexing, splitmecrackle crashmecriggle insane ass of a woman is practising howling below stairs with a brute of a singingmaster so horribly, that my head is nearly off.

SCROOBIOUS

scroobious dubious doubtfulness

SPONGETANEOUSLY

SPONGETANEOUSLY

. . . I can only offer you 4 small potatoes, some olives, 5 tomatoes, and a lot of castor oil berries. These, if mashed up with some crickets who have spongetaneously come to life in my cellar, may make a novel, if not nice or nutritious Jam or Jelley.

SILL KANKERCHIEF

Always put a Sill Kankerchief in your pocket in case of change of wind . . ,

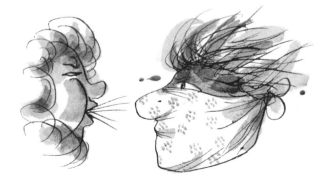

TED-BIME

T t

TED-BIME

It is . . . ted-bime.—Goodnight.

TENDA-NESS

. . . I have been a-walking over the Col di Tenda, which produced so to speak a Tenda-ness in my feet . . .

U u

UGLYISM

The new church is beginning: the beastliest uglyism you ever beheld—like a caterpillar with a cyclops's head.

USBING

I . . . have written to Lady Derby to know if she wants her usbing's hancester's picter.

V v

VEELS

. . . I nearly ran under the veels of her Chariot . . .

VULCHERS

I wen tup two the Zoological Gardings, & drew a lot of
Vulchers. . . .

WIOLENT

WIOLENT

. . . she is wiolent and spiteful, although hospitable.

WITCH

Witch fax I only came at granulously as it were—grain by grain, as the pigeon said when he picked up the bushel of corn slowly.

X x

. . . a truly good Xtian (Christian)

Y y

YERSELL

Noo, just tak cair of yersell . . .

Z z

Noa zur. (No sir.)